The Missing Gargoyle

of the Ladies' Library

Lois Richmond

Illustrated by Denise Lisiecki

Published in collaboration with
Fortitude Graphic Design & Printing and Season Press LLC.

Library of Congress Control Number: 2014956431

ISBN: 10-0-9741611-8-7
ISBN: 13-978-0-9741611-8-1

Richmond, Lois, 1935-The Missing Gargoyle of the Ladies' Library/ by Lois Richmond.

Summary: The gargoyle of the Ladies' Library Association, stolen from its place on

the building, shares of his experience in the hands of his assailant.

1.Gargoyle-History. 2. Ladies' Library Association-History. 3.Gargoyle theft-Historical Fiction

Denise Lisiecki used watercolor paints to create the illustrations for this book.

Printed in the United States of America

First Edition

10 9 8 7 6 5 4 3 2 1

This book is dedicated to the original gargoyle presented to the Ladies' Library Association and

its many years of service and the mystery he holds within. He serves as a sentry to the 1879

building and contents. Some believe his presence wards off bad spirits and

provides security and protection.

L.R.

The illustrations in this book are dedicated to my two Jacobs.

D.L.

ACKNOWLEDGEMENTS

I want to extend thanks to those who have helped make this book possible. To my husband, Jim and my son, Andrew for serving as models for the thief character. To my daughter, Emilie Richmond Ranzo, for sharing pictures of her cat Skittles who was the model for Rachel the cat. To the Ladies of the Ladies' Library Association who served as models for the tea scene in the book: Barbara Baker, June Cottrell, Rose Marie Coy and Marge Kars.

To Vic and Ruth Eichler, Mary Whalen and Judy Sherrod for technical advice. And to my grandsons Jarrod and Connor Wetzel Brown for their input on the story.

I want to thank Sharon Carlson, M. Stephen Doherty, Nelson Nave and Betty Lee Ongley for their advance reviews and praise. Also, thanks to Lynn Houghton of Western Michigan University Archives and Michigan Regional History, and *MLive* Editor Mickey Ciokajlo for help with the *Kalamazoo Gazette* articles published here to authenticate this story. And, thanks to Sonya and Sean Hollins (Fortitude Graphics and Season Press) for their assistance in the final design and publication of my first book.

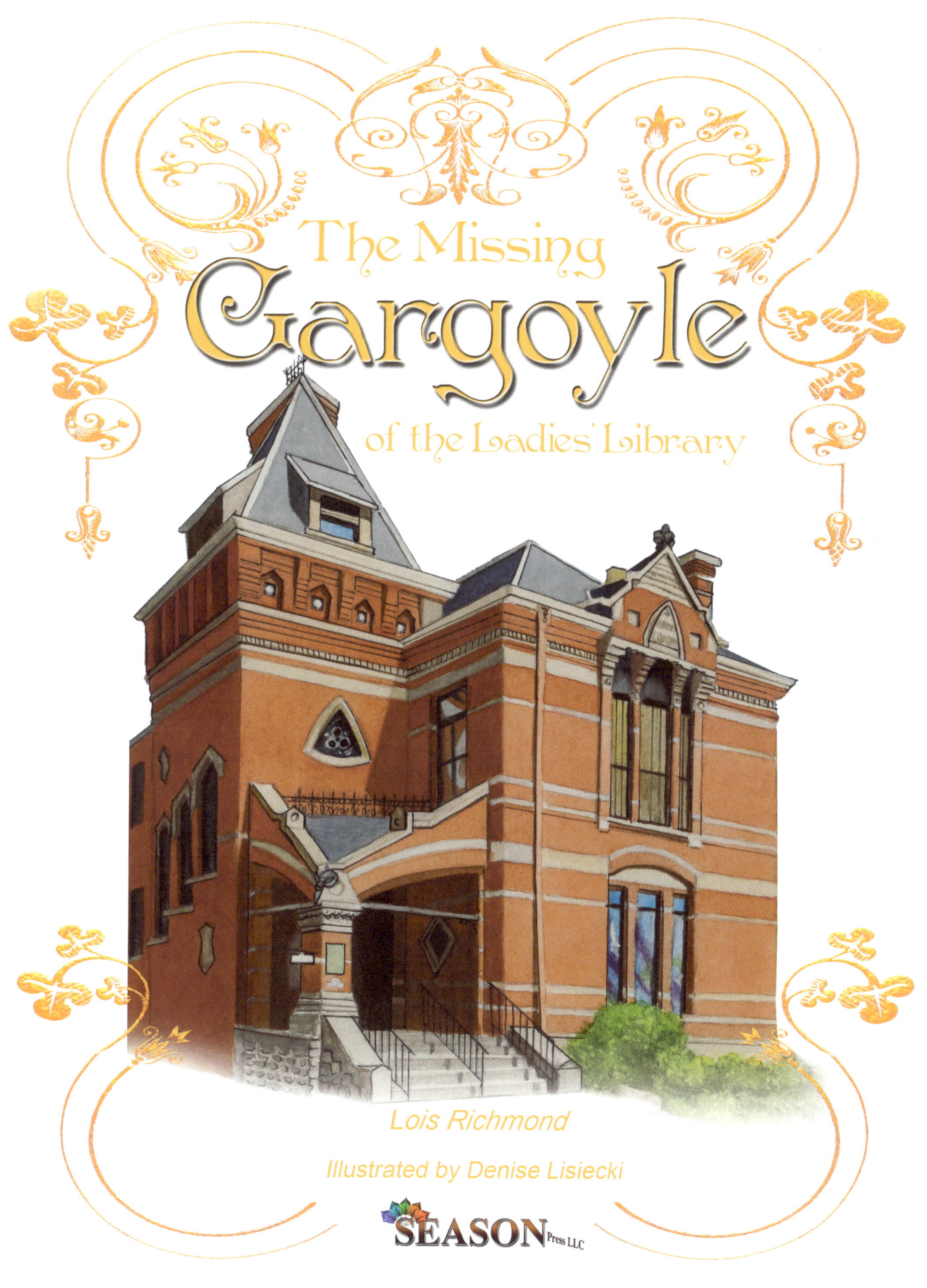

The Missing Gargoyle

of the Ladies' Library

Lois Richmond

Illustrated by Denise Lisiecki

SEASON Press LLC

 love the smell of fresh-baked cinnamon rolls and the activity that goes on frequently in this historic building. The Ladies enjoy it too as they discuss how to contribute to others in the community and carry on the many important club traditions. It warms my heart to hear the laughter and music that takes place among these old walls. I feel so safe surrounded by the most distinguished collection of books on the shelves near where I am perched. On the inside of this metal exterior, I am smiling. However, there was a time when my future with the Ladies' Library Association was in dire straits.

My history as a gargoyle waterspout at the Ladies' Library building began in 1904, when I was presented as a gift in honor of the new building. Waterspouts are famous in Europe. Many of my cousins in France are on monumental buildings. They have achieved notoriety for their role in draining water from the higher parts of buildings away from its structure to prevent damage to walls and basements. We gargoyles were once used on Egyptian temples to serve as waterspouts. We were even used in Pompeii and on Notre Dame de Paris. In the United States, we can be seen at such places as the Chrysler Building in New York City and Princeton University.

y dilemma began one dark, rainy and tad chilly morning. I was just doing my job when suddenly there was a man reaching for me. He began loosening my brackets. Something terrible was happening!

I had observed a tall lanky man riding a bicycle from time to time on Park Street. He often wore a yellow slicker and hat when it rained and frequently observed me, especially during rainstorms. I could see in the early light of dawn that this was the same man!

THE CIVIC
NOW SHOWING

e had borrowed a ladder that was left outside by one of the workers of the Civic Theatre next door. It was just high enough for him to reach me. As he removed the last bolt, he nearly fell backwards. He worked himself back down the ladder with me tightly gripped under his arm.

Maybe he was moving me. But why? I was doing a good job right here. Once down the ladder he quickly stuffed me in the gunnysack laying on the ground. He returned the ladder to the building next door and quickly tossed me over his shoulder and hopped on his rickety old bicycle. He wobbled a bit before managing to balance on the bike with one hand while holding the gunnysack with the other. We headed north down Park Street. I was frightened and angry. I was being stolen!

 kept thinking, why was this man taking me away? From the length of the ride we must have continued on outside of the city. It was not a good ride. I bounced along as his old bicycle wheels squeaked with every turn.

As we arrived at our destination, he let his old bicycle fall to the ground on its side. He laid me on the ground and took me out of the gunnysack. I could see a run-down shack covered partially with vines. The wood on the shack was old and showed only slight signs of white paint. The windows were smudged and the area looked rundown and rather unkempt. There was trash in the front yard alongside a puddle of water. The neighborhood was sparsely populated. It looked like a lonely place and I was frightened.

After spending many years on busy Park Street with lots of traffic, I was out here in the country with very little activity. I heard a rooster off in the distance, which only told me other homes were far away. I started to worry about how I was going to get back to the Ladies' Library— my home. I was the only gargoyle installed on a building in Kalamazoo. Being stuck out here at this shack was a real dilemma.

 s daylight approached, a passerby stopped for a brief visit. He called my thief, Elmer. The two spoke about the small shack and the problem it had with water damage. The old shack was made of wood and had a sloped porch. Beneath the porch was a gully where the water had formed the puddle. The old shack was in need of much repair.

Nearby, a big yellow cat sat quietly. Elmer called her Rachel and talked to her as if she were his best friend. He stood and rubbed his forehead as he pondered what to do next. Rachel's long tail moved slowly back and forth; puzzled that something was not right and she wasn't happy about it.

Elmer continued to talk to her about how he planned to anchor me to the corner of his house. She continued to act upset by moving her tail swiftly from side to side. He told her I would make a big improvement to the place and how he had watched me serve as a downspout for the Ladies' Library. He knew I would do a good job for his little shack. Elmer started calling me his "Gargo," and seemed proud to have taken me for his own. I was lonely and I knew Rachel realized I had been stolen.

Shortly after we arrived, a lady Elmer called Selma, stopped in and delivered a beautiful pink glossy cake on a white milk-glass pedestal. He waters her flowers in times of dry spells and she rewards him with the scrumptious Pink Lemonade cake. This gesture has been going on for years and it was a treat Elmer truly appreciated.

ack at the Library…

As Ladies arrived at the building one looked up and screamed, "The gargoyle is missing! Someone has taken him!" They were frantic and immediately went inside and tried to calm down so they could think of what to do next. They fixed tea, warmed cinnamon rolls, and continued their discussion of the missing gargoyle. Without him, the building would be in danger of water damage that could ruin their historic landmark.

What to do? What to do?

They called the police and reported the theft. The police suggested the Ladies first find a replacement for the gargoyle while they looked for the thief. They agreed with the need of a temporary solution for the waterspout.

One of the Ladies knew of a metalsmith by the name of Lee Wallace who lived in Portage. He would be able to help make a replica that could be used until their beloved gargoyle was found. They described the gargoyle to Mr. Wallace and showed him a photograph. He said recreating such an antique sculpture would be difficult, but he was up for the challenge. He told them this was not an easy task and would do his best. In the meantime, they called the custodian of the Library and asked that a piece of metal be bent and secured to the roof edge to channel any rainwater away from the side of the building. It was helpful, but it could not compare to the job the gargoyle had done.

ack at Elmer's…

It started to rain in drips and drizzles and then with steady force. As the water came off the sloped roof of the shack it was obvious I could handle it. Elmer praised me and told me how he appreciated the good work. Rachel sat nearby and listened. It was evident to her that I was lonely and did not feel good about this place. The shack could have had a piece of drainpipe to do this job; not a fancy gargoyle like me! I was fashioned to grace a fancy building not an old wooden shack!

Later in the evening, Elmer heard the local news on his radio. The announcer said: **We have sad news to report. Yesterday, the gargoyle on the Ladies' Library building at 333 South Park Street was stolen. This important waterspout was purchased in England and was a gift given to the Ladies to use on their historic building. A reward is being offered by the Ladies for its safe return. Anyone with information is asked to call the police. In other news…**

Both Elmer and Rachel heard the news report. I knew Elmer's conscience was telling him he needed to return me to my home. He knew he was a thief and he would be in big trouble with the law if he did not take me back. I heard him mumble to Rachel, "I like Gargo right here and I have no intentions of returning him anytime soon!" Rachel sat quietly, but her tail moved ever so slowly as a sure sign she was in deep thought and contemplating what to do next.

hen they went into the house Elmer sat in his favorite chair and Rachel placed her paws upon the edge of his chair. She looked Elmer straight in the face and he could almost hear her say, "If you do not return the gargoyle I will no longer live here!" Her disgust was obvious.

Elmer knew Rachel could find another home because she was a good cat and kept mice under control. There were mice that lived in the shack and Rachel kept them from eating the food— especially the Pink Lemonade cake. Just then, a couple of mice scurried around the cake that sat on the small wooden table. They decided to sample a few crumbs. Usually Rachel would get after them, but instead she just sat and watched. Elmer called out, "Rachel, get 'em, they are eating my cake!"

But she did not move. Rachel often served as Elmer's conscience and she knew what he had to do. In the meantime, the mice were delighted that Rachel gave them a break and let them enjoy some of the wonderful cake.

She let Elmer know by her actions that she would let the mice eat all of the cake if he did not follow his conscience and return the stolen gargoyle.

Rachel's actions were a concern to Elmer. He could not bear to have her leave. Elmer thought about his predicament and how he first felt it was okay to move me from my home. But now his conscience was bothering him. He was a thief!

ater, on that dark seemingly moonless night, Elmer could not sleep. He tossed and turned knowing what he had done was wrong. He needed to think about his future. This was against everything his mother had taught him. Besides, he loved Pink Lemonade cake and couldn't bear the thought of the mice continuing to eat away at it. Even more, he loved Rachel and didn't want to see her go.

One year later...

I have watched the seasons come and go and I feel so useless in this place. Being happy in what you do is very important. My job at the Ladies' Library gave me many rewards and satisfaction and I am anxious to return to my home. The piece of metal sheet was still trying to work as a downspout while Mr. Wallace worked on my replica.

As Selma continued to bring over her Pink Lemonade cake, the mice enjoyed eating their share. Rachel continued to turn her back on the mice when they were feasting, in hopes Elmer would come to his senses. Suddenly, he could not stand it anymore. He had had enough!

n the still of the darkness, he took me down from the corner of his shack. In his haste he slightly disassembled some of my parts, which caused me to be broken into three large pieces. He placed me, and all of my parts, into the gunnysack and jumped on his old bicycle. It was a dreadful ride as we bounced along in the thick of the rainy night. Soon we were headed south on Park Street.

When we arrived back at the Ladies' Library building, he removed me from the gunnysack and placed me in a wooden crate that was on the porch. As I sat on the porch waiting to be discovered, I watched as the makeshift metal spout tried miserably to do my job. I was so glad to be back in my neighborhood and anxious for the Ladies to find me.

The next morning, some of the Ladies arrived early and were stunned and amazed to find me on the porch in the crate. Elmer had attached a note, which said he was sorry and knew I should be returned. They were thankful and excited that I was back home because they loved me. They were sad to see me in three pieces but knew I could be fixed. They also thought that maybe, I deserved a safer place inside the building. I was a one-of-a kind gargoyle that really could not be replaced.

333
CLUB
HIGAN

all Bequest

hey were so pleased that I was returned that they asked the police to stop the search for the thief. When Mr. Wallace completed my replica it was placed in my old spot above the porch. As for me, one Lady suggested hiring Corwin Rife, of the Kalamazoo Public Museum, to repair me so I could be useful again. He was able to fasten and secure me back together.

I am loved and admired daily for the many years I served as a downspout. But today, I am inside the Library where I am placed on a hook behind the entry door. I sit high as a sentry to watch over the interior and the decor of books, paintings and statuary that were purchased in Europe. You may come and visit me at 333 South Park Street in Kalamazoo, Michigan...the home of the Ladies' Library Association.

As the Ladies celebrate my history, I know Rachel is happy back at the shack with Elmer, Selma and their Pink Lemonade cake. Elmer thanked Rachel for encouraging him to do the right thing and he vowed never to steal again.

The End

Factual History Of The Ladies' Library Association & The Library Gargoyle

In 1844, women in Kalamazoo, Michigan sought to educate themselves and learn to read. Since women were expected to be productive (cooking, cleaning and raising children), reading was not considered required or necessary. However, they held reading groups disguised as sewing clubs where women learned together.

Books became very important to them and led to the accumulation of enough books to start the first circulating library in Kalamazoo. Eight women, one of whom was Dr. Lucinda Stone, led this effort. Known as the "Mother of Women's Clubs," Dr. Stone was the wife of the president of Kalamazoo College, which was established in 1833. As an educator, she made numerous trips to Europe where she purchased pictures and statuary to share and teach others. Most of these art objects still adorn the Ladies' Library building.

As the books accumulated, storage and space became an issue and led to the group changing locations several times. In 1852, the women established the Ladies Library Association (LLA) as the first women's club in the state of Michigan, and the third in the United States. In 1879, after many years of difficulty and obstacles, they managed to design, build and solely own the first building established by a women's organization in the United States. The LLA was designated as Michigan Historical Commission Registered Site No.221 in 1961.

This magnificent building is still the home of the association, which thrives today with approximately 200 members. Like the Ladies who founded the organization, the women today still devote their time to enrich the lives of others through education, literacy, philanthropy and volunteerism. Their mission also includes preserving the building, its contents, traditions and the National Historic designation it received in 1970. Their motto continues to be, "Do What You Can."

Based on the discussion in the association's 1880 meeting minutes, some believe the gargoyle was installed on the building in 1879; however, photos do not substantiate this claim. It was later believed that Anna D. Clark purchased the gargoyle in England and donated it to the LLA in 1904. The LLA gargoyle is believed to be the only one installed on a building in Kalamazoo. The conflicting dates of the gargoyle's existence at LLA adds mystery and interest to the already Gothic-style structure built in 1879. In architecture a gargoyle is usually a carved animal, human or bird grotesque in appearance. They are designed with a spout that conveys water from the roof of a structure and away from its sides to prevent rainwater from running along the outside walls and damaging the masonry or wood.

The term gargoyle comes from the French word, *gargoville*, which in English means throat or gullet. Similar words from the word root gar, means "to swallow," which represents the gurgling sound of water. When not constructed as a waterspout, some gargoyles are considered sculptures.

In addition, they are believed to frighten off bad spirits and protect those it guards. Gargoyles were used mainly in Europe into the early 18th Century before drainpipes were substituted to carry the water to the ground.

In 1962, the *Kalamazoo Gazette*, published three articles pertaining to the missing gargoyle that was stolen in 1961, and its mysterious return (in three pieces) a year later. Some believe college students may have reached him by standing on top of a car; but this was never proven. After more than sixty years, no one has ever claimed responsibility for the disappearance or return of the gargoyle. It remains a mystery that only the gargoyle knows.

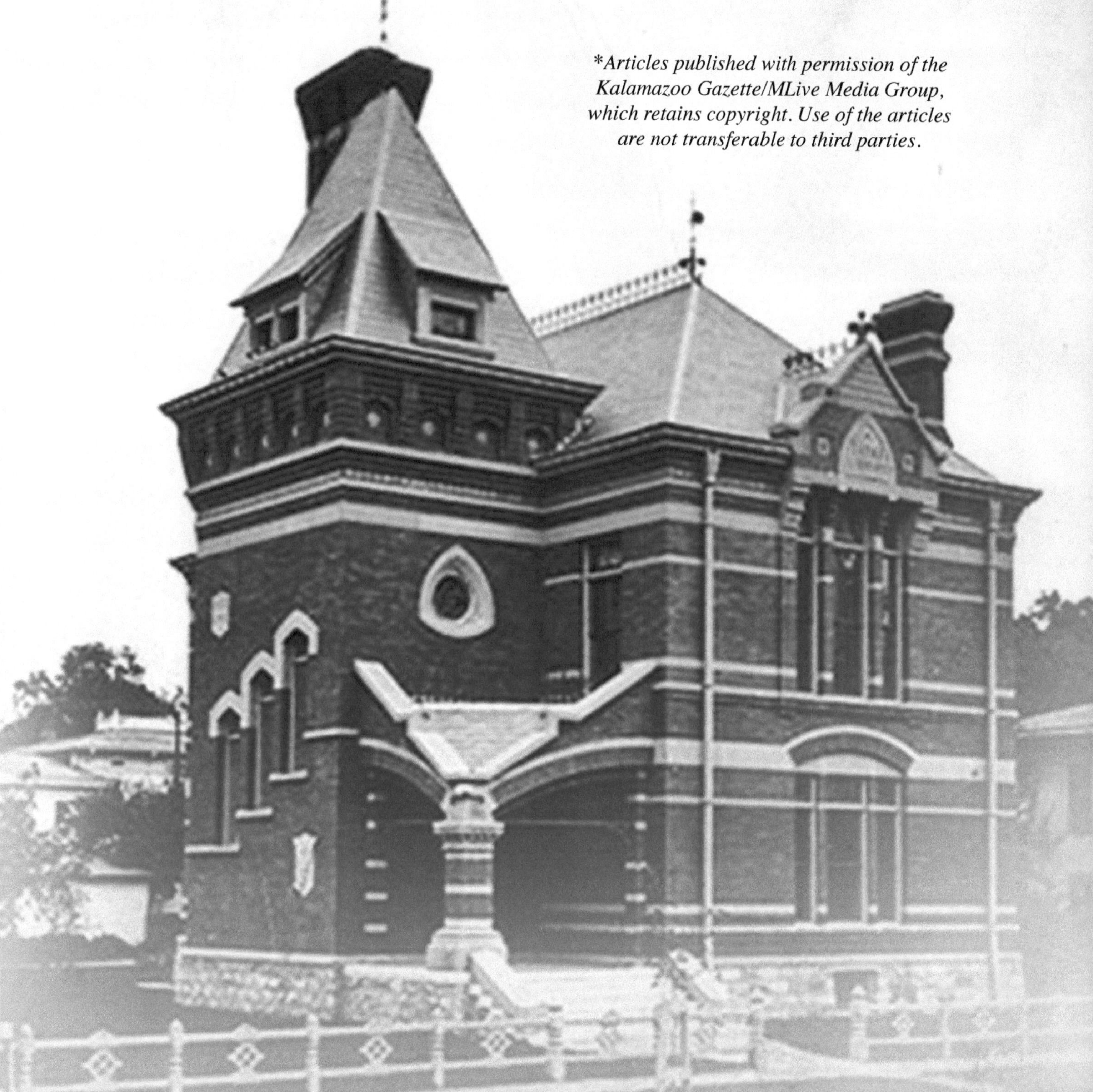

One is an antique

JUL23 1978

WHICH IS THE 'REAL' GARGOYLE? Actually both are "real," but one is a copy of the other. (Does this help in picking out the original and the copy?) The original, bottom, "rests" in a place of honor inside the Ladies Library Association building at 333 S. Park. It has been inside ever since it was stolen and damaged some years back. Returned to the LLA (no questions asked), it was repaired and placed inside the building. The exact age of the original is unknown, but during the 1880s it was mentioned in the LLA's minutes. The "new" gargoyle, in the likeness of the original, can be seen "at work" outside the building. For those unfamiliar with "their work," gargoyles are suppose to be hideous creatures whose job is to serve as a rain spout, projecting from the gutter of a building. The copy was done by Lee Wallace of Portage, whose work was featured in a Gazette article in February. Wallace handsculptured the new piece in copper.

MUSEUM EMPLOYES CHECK GARGOYLE
Corwin Rife Shows Marilyn Hartsell Repairs Needed
—Gazette photo

Going Home Soon

Ladies Library Association Gargoyle Getting Repairs

The gargoyle stolen last August from the Ladies Library Association building at 333 S. Park is undergoing repairs and may be b a c k in place a year after its theft.

The gargoyle lost a leg and an ear some time since it was last seen in its place on the building, but the broken parts w e r e included in a wooden crate in which the gargoyle was returned last month to the porch of the building from which it was gargoyle-naped.

Corwin Rife, curator of exhibits at the Kalamazoo Public Museum, is repairing the decorated waterspout for the Ladies Library Association. He estimates it will take him about a month of part-time work to prepare the gargoyle for its return to duty at the bottom of the roof.

The gargoyle probably is the only one in Kalamazoo, according to museum director Alexis Praus.

Mrs. Loren Phelps, president of the Ladies Library, says a note in the crate said that whoever returned it felt

who took it," Mrs. Phelps adds.

A former president of the association, Mrs. C a r l C. Blankenburg, remembers the gargoyle before it was placed on a corner of the building.

Mrs. Blankenburg says the gargoyle was brought to Kalamazoo from England by Miss Anna D. Clark, who was dean of girls at Central High School.

"Miss Clark had t h e gargoyle on her desk for awhile and then presented it to the Ladies Library Association in, I believe, the fall of 1904."

The zinc gargoyle is about 18 inches tall. The building on which it was placed was the first in the United States to be built and owned by a women's club.

Encyclopedia Brittanica reports the general use of the word gargoyle has become restricted to the grotesque, carved rainspouts of the middle ages.

T H E GARGOYLE of the developed Gothic period — which is what the Ladies Li-

the roof and eaves rolls from its outstretched tongue.

The gargoyle was part of a building known as eclectic architecture which "takes the best of all architecture and adds some of its own," Praus says.

Another example of t h a t style, he adds, is the People's Church at 341 W. Lovell, a Unitarian-Universalist church.

The w o r d gargoyle is derived from a Gothic description of the gurgling s o u n d made by running water. The word gargle has the same derivation.

The gargoyle's owner was organized in 1852 as the third oldest women's club in the nation and the oldest in Michigan.

The group's purpose was to establish and maintain a circulating library and promote literary culture. It brought such speakers to Kalamazoo as authors Horace Greeley, Wendell Phillips and Bayard Taylor.

Kalamazoo's only circulation library at its formation, it also was the town's only li-

SEP 7 1961

Gargoyle Stolen from Ladies Library Building

Believed to be the only one in Kalamazoo, the green gargoyle atop the column of the historic Ladies Library Association, 333 S. Park, has been stolen.

The gargoyle, hand-carved from stone, is 18 inches long and eight inches square. It's use was as a rainspout — a use traced to Egyptian architecture.

The gargoyle was placed on the building in 1878, the year the building was erected for the then fabulous sum of $14,000. The building was the first in the United States to be built and owned by a women's club.

* * *

ASSOCIATION members said the copper wire holding the gargoyle was cut within the past three weeks and the two bolts removed, presumably by pranksters standing on the top of a car.

It was called probably the only gargoyle in Kalamazoo by Alexis Praus, director of Kalamazoo's Public Museum.

The word gargoyle is derived from a Gothic description of the gurgling sound of running water. The word gargle has the same derivation. Rain ran from the gargoyle's carved tongue.

The gargoyle was part of a building known as eclectic architecture, which "takes the best of all architecture and adds some of its own," Praus said. Another example of that style is the First Presbyterian Church, he added.

The association hadn't noticed the gargoyle missing until this week, members said today, because the group doesn't meet during the summer months.

* * *

THE ASSOCIATION was organized in 1852, making it the third oldest women's club in the U.S., the oldest in Michigan. The group's purpose was to establish and maintain a circulating library and promote literary culture. To this purpose, it brought such speakers to Kalamazoo as authors Horace Greeley, Wendell Phillips, and Bayard Taylor. Kalamazoo's only circulation library at its formation, it also was the town's only library for many years.

The building was named a state historical site by the State Historical Commission last spring.

Pink Lemonade Cake

Makes 1 Bundt cake
Ability - Easy

Ingredients:
Cake:
Butter or cooking spray for coating a Bundt pan.
1 18.25-ounce white cake mix plus any other ingredients the package directions call for.
3 Tablespoons pink lemonade drink powder.
1 teaspoon finely grated lemon zest (add more for more lemon taste).

Creamy Glaze:
2 cups confectioners' sugar
1/3-cup butter or margarine
1 1/2 teaspoon vanilla
2 -4 Tablespoons hot water
Red food coloring

Directions:

Preheat oven to 350° F. Butter or spray the Bundt pan.

Cake: In a large bowl, stir together the cake mix and lemonade powder. Prepare the cake batter according to the package directions, using any additional ingredients called for (eggs, milk, water, oil, etc.). Stir the lemon zest into the batter. Pour the batter into the prepared pan.

Bake 30 to 40 minutes or until golden. Let the cake cool for 10-15 minutes. Carefully turn cake out onto a cake stand to cool completely.

Glaze: Melt butter or margarine in saucepan, blend in sugar and vanilla, stir in water 1 tablespoon at a time until glaze is of proper consistency. Add 1 drop at a time of red food coloring until you have the pink color you prefer. Drizzle the pink glaze carefully over the top and allow to run down the sides.

THE AUTHOR

Lois Richmond joined the Ladies' Library Association in 2002, and served as the organization's president from 2012-2014. It was during that time she became fascinated with the history of the organization's mascot gargoyle and its actual disappearance. In honor of the $1.5 million renovations of the Ladies' Library Association (in 2013) Lois celebrates the gargoyle and his decades-long history as an iconic fixture in this, her debut book.

Lois was born and raised in Richland, Michigan. She attended Bronson School of Nursing and Western Michigan University in nearby Kalamazoo where she earned a Bachelor of Science degree. After more than thirty years as a nurse at Bronson Hospital in Kalamazoo, she retired as assistant director of nursing administration. She enjoys many hobbies, and the self-taught naturalist has held nature classes for adults at her private nature preserve.

THE ILLUSTRATOR

Denise Lisiecki was born in Cleveland, Ohio. She earned a Bachelor's of Fine Arts from Miami University, and a master's degree from the State University of New York. She also attended the University of North Dakota, Kent State and Cleveland State University.

Her works have been featured in more than forty individual exhibitions, more than 100 group exhibitions and are represented in more than sixty museums and corporate collections. She is one of only two painters in Michigan to be awarded the National Endowment for the Arts Midwest Fellowship.

Denise has received two Creative Artists grants from the Michigan Council for the Arts and was selected to represent the Midwest with two of her paintings for the exhibition, *Sea to Shining Sea*, curated by Haggin Museum in Stockton, California.

Her paintings are reproduced in such books and magazines as *Sea to Shining Sea* (Haggin Museum); *Daily Life in Still Life* by Lynn Moss; *Easy Solutions: Color Mixing* by Stephen Doherty; *Denise Lisiecki: Choosing Still-Life Objects for Their Meaning* by Stephen Doherty; *Watercolor Magazine*, *From Screen Printing to Painting and Back* by Ruthe Thompson; *American Artist Magazine*, *Denise Lisiecki: Serigraphs of Female Sensibility* by Ruthe Thompson, and *Screen Printing Magazine*.

Denise has been a guest lecturer, adjunct professor, workshop instructor and national juror. Presently, she is Director of the Kirk Newman Art School at the Kalamazoo Institute of Arts.

Learn more about her at: www.kazoopainter.com